SOPHIE WASHINGTON
THE GAMER

WRITTEN BY
TONYA DUNCAN ELLIS

D1113728

Books By
Tonya Duncan Ellis

Sophie Washington: Queen of the Bee

Sophie Washington: The Snitch

Sophie Washington:
Things You Didn't Know About Sophie

Sophie Washington: The Gamer

Sophie Washington: Hurricane

Table of Contents

Chapter 1

Sunday Service

"The Lord bless you and keep you;
The Lord make his face shine on you
And be gracious to you;
The Lord turn his face toward you
And give you peace.
Amen."

I lift my head up from prayer and my eight-year-old brother, Cole, grumbles, "I'm starving," as we hustle out of the crowded church.

New Faith Church is one of the largest Baptist churches in Houston. I love coming with my dad, mom and little brother each week, and it looks like the entire congregation showed up today. During the service we were squished in our seats like sardines, and Mom had to put her purse on the floor to make room. I spot my best friend Chloe in the row across from us. She and her family have been attending New Faith since she was little, just like we have.

"Hey Sophie," she waves. "I love your dress!"

I smooth the skirt of my floral print, blue and white dress. Mom bought it for me last week and I love to twirl around in it. Chloe looks beautiful herself, as usual, wearing a light-yellow sweater dress and grown-up looking shoes with a small heel. Tall, with curly black hair and a bright smile, Chloe is one of the prettiest girls my class.

Now that I am getting older and am in the sixth grade, I can understand more of what our pastor is saying in the sermons. Today, he was talking about how hard it can be to stay away from things we like that may be bad for us.

"Temptation is a daily struggle for all," he preached.

"The struggle for me is staying awake for two hours," complains Cole. "I wish I could have been with my friends in children's church."

Cole prefers going to the special service for kids, and was mad that Mom and Dad made us join them in the main church this morning.

"It's getting closer to Easter, and I want you to get a better understanding of what the holiday is all about," Dad explains. "In children's church, all you pay attention to is the snacks."

"Those donuts they bring in are good!" Cole exclaims.

"Maybe we can stop by the donut shop on the way home." Mom squeezes his shoulder.

I roll my eyes. Since Cole is the youngest, he's my mother's pet.

"Have you kids given any thought as to what you want to give up for Lent?" Dad asks.

"What's Lent?" questions Cole.

"Lent represents the 40 days Jesus was in the desert and the devil tried to tempt him, or get him to do things he shouldn't do," Mom explains. "During the 40 days before Easter, we celebrate Lent by giving up something we like to eat or do that keeps us from thinking of more meaningful things, just like Jesus did."

"Oh yeah, I remember when we did this last year," Cole recalls. "I stopped watching cartoons. This time, I'm giving up eating vegetables."

"But that's not something you like!" I laugh.

"I do like *some* vegetables," he refutes, "just not all of them."

"Well, giving up something that you don't care much for defeats the purpose of observing Lent," Mom says to my brother. "The point is learning to resist temptation and focus on God."

"And I've never seen you willingly eat any vegetable," I chime in. "Just last week you hid your broccoli under the placemat when Mom and Dad weren't looking."

"Thanks for squealing, Tattletale," accuses Cole.

"I can't wait until Easter," I say, changing the subject. "Will we get new outfits?"

"P-leease don't make me wear short pants and a sweater vest again this year!" my brother begs.

"I guess we could go Easter shopping next weekend," Mom replies. "Cole, you are probably old enough to get a suit."

"Not shopping again!" he groans. "I can't stand going to the mall."

"I wonder if they will have a spring festival at school this year." I think aloud.

The Xavier Spring Spectacular is a huge fund-raising event with food, games, prizes and music that comes around before Easter.

Last year, Cole won a baby chick that lived for about a month before it wandered out of our garage, never to be seen again.

We get in our car to head home.

"Bleep, bleep, bleep," I hear as we start to drive off.

"Cole, don't tell me you brought that game to church with us!" frowns Mom.

"I just need to finish one more level," he says, looking intently at the screen of his Nintendo DS, hand-held video game player.

My little brother is obsessed with video games. His favorite is a game called Video Rangers that has lots of weird characters trying to take over the universe. He has a Video Rangers guide book that lists hundreds of video ranger fighters, which he has practically memorized. Lately, he's been spending every spare minute playing his game. I bet he hears that *bleep, bleep* sound in his sleep.

"Turn that nonsense off, son," commands Dad from the driver's seat.

"Okay, I just need to get Megazor to a safe place." Cole continues to move the joystick on his game.

Mom swivels her head to look in the backseat of the car in surprise, and I see Dad's expression turn thunderous. He doesn't take lightly to us not doing as he asks.

"I said turn that thing off, young man!" he sternly repeats.

Cole flips off the power switch to his game and looks sheepish.

"Looks like we've figured out what you should give up for Lent, Cole," says Mom. "Video games.

Chapter 2

Lent

"That's not fair!" Cole exclaims. "I don't want to give up my games for Lent."

"I've been concerned about the amount of time you spend playing video games, son," Mom gently replies. "The minute you get in the car you start playing, and I see you on them almost every day after school and on weekends. This may be a good time for you to put them aside for a while and do other things.

"Lent officially begins this Wednesday," she continues, "so you can prepare yourself to take a break in the meantime."

"Your mother is right," Dad chimes in. "Your grades have gone down some, and we blame the time you are wasting playing video games. And I haven't seen you doing any of your drawings in weeks."

Cole is great in art, and used to spend time drawing after school every day. When people see his pictures, they sometimes think a high schooler made them. Last year, one of Cole's drawings of a pair of cowboy boots won a first-place ribbon in the state rodeo art contest.

After our parents finish speaking he sits stunned in the back seat with his lip poked out.

"It's not like it's the end of the world, Cole," I chide. "It's just 40 days, and they're just some silly video games."

"You don't understand," he groans. "I'm the leader of my ranger pack, and I have a 100-day streak going. If I stop playing, I will lose everything!"

Tears roll down Cole's face. Dad shakes his head.

"Your outburst convinces me that we are doing the right thing in having you put these games down for a bit," says Dad. "This is getting out of control."

We head into the house and Cole stomps up to his room. Twenty minutes later, I go upstairs to find him, and he is back at it with the video games on the television in our family game room. This time he playing the NBA basketball game he got for his birthday, and has headphones on his ears.

"Rebound the ball, Bozo! You are trash!!" he yells at the screen.

"Dang bro, that was harsh!" I exclaim, pulling down his earplugs.

"Get out of here, Creep," he looks up. "Lent doesn't start until Wednesday, and I'm getting all the playing I can get in while I can."

"Are you playing with someone else?" I ask.

"It's Carlos, from school," he replies. "He's on my team."

Cole puts his headphones back, moves his hands on his joystick and tunes me out.

"I said, fake to the left! Your moves are garbage, man!"

This really is crazy. No wonder Mom and Dad are making him put up the video games.

I'm surprised Cole has been allowed to play his games for so long in the first place. My parents won't even let me get a cell phone, and I'm in middle school. This past Fall they almost gave in, and had bought me a phone they were going to give me for my birthday. But before I found out about my gift, I sneaked and borrowed a phone from a kid in our neighborhood. I got in trouble in school with it, so my parents say I have to wait until I am more mature before they buy me my own phone. Cole, on the other hand, gets away with murder, because he's "Mommy's Little Baby." When I was his age, I was lucky to get a set of blocks, let alone two video game systems!

When I think about it, Cole has been playing his video games almost non-stop for weeks. Mom and Dad have been so busy working at Dad's dental office that they haven't seen what was going on. We had a flood here in Houston a few months ago, and water ruined Dad's office. While it was getting repaired, Mom spent a lot of time helping out at the dental practice, and Cole and I went to after-care at school. Instead of doing homework in the after-school study hall, he sat with his friends playing video games. Now it's like he can't stop.

"Mom, Dad, Cole is playing his games again!" I run downstairs to tattle.

My parents are sitting at the kitchen table looking through some bills.

"Thanks for telling us what's going on, Sophie," says Dad, looking up. "but we told your brother that he had until the start of Lent to put his games away. Let's give him some time to get used to the idea. Have you thought about what you might want to give up for Lent?"

I'd been so busy worrying about Cole, I really hadn't considered it.

"What about tattling and complaining?" suggests Mom. "I'm trying to give up thinking negatively, myself."

"It's no fair!" I begin to grumble again. "I can't even get a cell phone, and I'm in the sixth grade, yet Cole plays video games from sunrise to sunset and you do nothing.

"A point well taken," Dad responds, "Which is why we are having Cole put up his games for Lent in a couple of days. In the meantime, you thinking about putting the brakes on some of your grumbling for a while might be a good idea as well."

I leave the kitchen and head to the family room to watch some television. As usual, the focus is more on what I am doing wrong than what Cole needs to do. I can't wait until Wednesday to see what happens when his precious games are taken away.

Chapter 3

Birthday Surprise

Over the weekend, I agree with my parents to give up tattling and complaining. On the way to school Monday morning, I realize that this will be harder than I thought.

"Mom, what does it mean when clouds are low in the sky?" asks Cole.

"I'm not sure, Honey," says Mom. "I believe I read somewhere that it allows the earth to cool."

We drive along for a few more minutes and I start to doze. Then Cole pokes me with his elbow.

"How many different colors are there in a rainbow?"

"Google it," I mutter. "How am I supposed to know?"

"Now Sophie, be nice to your brother," scolds Mom. "It's good he's trying to understand the environment. Maybe you should look up the answer with him this afternoon after school."

"Just what I need, more homework," I sigh.

"Remember your Lent commitment," reminds Mom.

"Well, like Cole says with his video games, it doesn't officially begin until Wednesday," I reply, grabbing my backpack.

We pull up to our school and my mom pats my shoulder as we get out of the car.

"Be on time at pickup, because you and Cole have a dentist appointment after school," she reminds me.

"I hope they give me chocolate toothpaste!" chirps Cole.

I feel like whining about how much I hate getting my teeth cleaned, but remember my promise for Lent.

Since Xavier Academy is private and doesn't have a school bus, Mom drives us each morning and picks us up each afternoon. I sometimes get tired of having to wear uniforms every day and follow so many rules, but I like seeing all my friends and most of my teachers are pretty nice.

Cole heads toward the entrance of the lower school and I go through the main door of the middle school building.

As I round the corner by my locker I nearly bump into Toby Johnson.

"Hey Sophie, what's up?" Toby gives me a dimpled smile.

Earlier in the year, I had a serious crush on Toby and was nervous every time he was around. He moved to our school from Cleveland, and is uber cute with a curly afro, big brown eyes and a dimple on one cheek. In the past couple of months, we've become good friends, and I feel more comfortable around him.

"Hi Toby. Did you do anything fun this weekend?"

"Just the same old, same old," he replies. "My brother Michael had a basketball game, so we went to that, and my parents took us to the movies on Sunday to see *Snake Island*."

"How was it?" I ask. "I'm scared to see that."

"Sophie!" my best friend Chloe interrupts us, "get over here quick."

She motions me to her locker.

"See you later, Toby." I make my way down the hall.

As usual, Chloe looks like she just stepped out of a *Land's End* school catalog. Her curly, black hair is shiny and bouncy around her caramel skin, and she is carrying the cutest backpack with her initials sewn on it. I used to be jealous of Chloe because she is so pretty, but she is as nice as she is beautiful, so it's hard not to love her.

"Tomorrow is Mariama's birthday, and I thought of the perfect present for her!" she exclaims.

Mariama is another good friend of ours who moved to our school last year from Nigeria. She wears cool African dresses, and sometimes brings us neat desserts that her mom makes called puff puffs that look like spongy balls, and taste kind of like donuts.

"Since Tuesday will also be Mardi Gras," continues Chloe, "my mom is going to let me bring Mariama a King cake. We can decorate her locker with Mardi Gras beads and a birthday card. We have to get here early so we can have everything ready before she gets to school. It will be a surprise, so don't tell her."

"That sounds really nice," I say.

Chloe's family is from Louisiana, and they go all out with the Mardi Gras celebrations every year. Mardi Gras comes on the Tuesday before Lent begins. People eat and have parties to get ready for all they will be giving up on Lent. King cakes are yummy round cakes filled with cinnamon and sugar. They put a small plastic baby toy inside each cake, and if you find it, it means good luck. A couple of years ago, Chloe missed school for Mardi Gras because her family went to the big celebration in New Orleans. Her parents got to ride on one of the Mardi Gras floats with her aunts, and she had tons of Mardi Gras beads.

"I can bring all the supplies," she says. "I just need you to show up early to school so we can get things ready."

"Okay, I'll tell my mom," I say.

When I turned 11 a few months ago, Chloe barely said "Happy Birthday" to me, let alone planned a special surprise. But since I'm giving up complaining for Lent, I decide not to say anything.

"See you at lunch," I say as I make my way to first-period class.

"Okay, see you later!" she smiles.

Chapter 4

Cavity Creeps

Mom was waiting to pick us up right after school and I told her about Chloe's birthday plans for Mariama.

"That's very sweet of you two," she says. "Make sure you get down on time for breakfast and we can leave a little earlier."

"I wish I could have gone to after-care today," Cole groans. "I don't want to go to the dentist."

"That's just 'cause you want to play video games with Carlos," I say.

"I thought you agreed to give up games for Lent," says Mom.

"Lent doesn't begin until Wednesday," he replies, looking through the pouch in the car's backseat for his DS.

"Where's my game, Mom?"

"I took it out of the car to get you ready," she said. "You need to start scaling things down with the video games."

"You should throw all that junk out," I say.

"Leave me alone," Cole retorts. "You're just mad because we are going to the dentist and you are a Cavity Creep."

I punch him in the shoulder.

"Sophie! Cole!" Mom exclaims. "That's enough."

We pull into the parking lot of Dr. Patch, our dentist's office. Our dad is a dentist for adults, but Dr. Patch specializes in kids. She is really nice, and her office is decorated like a pirate ship. Murals of pirates, parrots and the ocean cover the walls. Next to the waiting room is a space filled with rainbow colored bean bags and a huge movie screen where you can watch cartoon movies before they call you back to get your teeth cleaned. In the actual office they have flat-screen TVs on the ceiling and headphones so you can watch while they are checking your teeth. Once you are done, you get a goody bag with a new toothbrush, paste and floss, and get to pick out a toy from Dr. Patch's treasure chest.

I thought all this was well and good until last year when I got my first cavity. I've had cavities before that Dr. Patch left alone since they were baby teeth and would fall out, but because this was a tooth in the back of my mouth that will stay until I'm at least 13, she said I needed to get it filled. I hated feeling them drill in my tooth to put the filling in, and I had to keep cotton in my mouth for about an hour while it dried, which was pretty uncomfortable. Cole laughed at me and said I looked like a Cavity Creep monster for days. I can't figure out how he doesn't have any cavities. Half the time he doesn't brush his teeth before bed, and his front teeth are as yellow as the sun.

"What flavor toothpaste would you like?" the dental hygienist asks before getting ready to clean my teeth.

"Do you have bubblegum?"

"You've been doing a great job at cleaning," she says as she pulls out the paste and uses an electric toothbrush to scrub my teeth. I try to ignore the whirring sound of the cleaning tool, and close my eyes to keep water and paste from splashing in them. After just a few minutes, she flosses me and I am finished with the worst part much quicker than I expected.

Next, Dr. Patch comes in and Mom follows. She had been in the other examining room with Cole.

"Let's see what we've got here," Dr. Patch says, looking in my open mouth. "Things look great, Mom. This little lady has been doing a good job at brushing. She has a couple more baby teeth to lose and we can start talking about braces."

"Braces?!" I exclaim, almost biting Dr. Patch's hand. "I don't want to be a brace face."

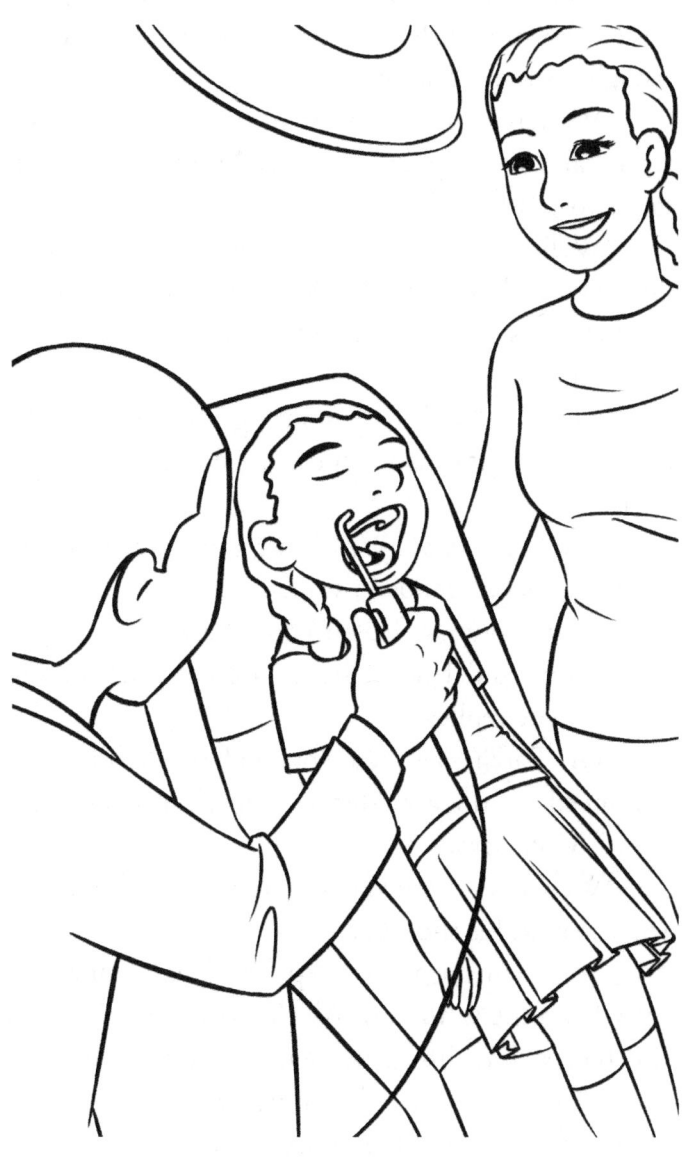

"You have beautiful teeth," Dr. Patch replies, "but a few of your lower front teeth are not quite as straight as they could be."

"We have a few months until your other baby teeth fall out, Sophie," soothes Mom, "so we can talk about it later."

"Well, the good news is that you don't have any cavities," says Dr. Patch. "You can head to my treasure chest for a prize, and we'll see you in about six months."

"That's why I hate coming to the dentist's office," I grumble as we move to the treasure chest area.

Cole has already picked out a green and yellow bouncing ball. I choose a slinky.

"How did your checkup go?" I ask.

"Okay, and I don't have to come back for six months," he replies.

"Dr. Patch says that you had two cavities, so you need to do a better job at cleaning, young man," Mom says.

"Welcome to the Cavity Creep club." I put my arms around his shoulder.

"You're just a plain creep," he laughs, hopping away from me to the car. All the way home he blips and bleeps with his game that he found under the seat. Mom is distracted talking with Dad on the phone about something going on at his office, and doesn't realize what is going on. It doesn't look like Cole is slowing down his playing like our parents asked him to. I feel like tattling on him, but clamp my mouth shut. They told me to stop complaining, didn't they?

Chapter 5

Mardi Gras

Tuesday morning I can't wait to get to school.

I wonder what Chloe will have to put on Mariama's locker?

That girl loves to decorate. Purple and teal striped wallpaper, a mini chandelier that lights up, and even a small lavender carpet jazz up her locker. My mom let me get some cute magnets and a mirror for my locker this year, but said that all the extras some of my classmates have are a bit over the top. I don't think any of the boys in the class have much in their lockers except maybe pictures of sports players.

"Yay! You made it extra early!!"

Chloe runs to give me a hug. I see the bag at her ankles.

"Let's get started."

She pulls out a gold poster that has "Happy Birthday and All That Jazz" written on it in green letters, and some cutouts of a saxophone and a trumpet that I display on the locker. Next, we stick on colorful Mardi Gras beads, balloons and a cool purple mask that has purple, green and gold feathers on it.

"She'll love it!" I exclaim.

"What are all the decorations for?" asks Nathan Jones, another of our classmates walking up the hall. "Whose birthday is it?"

"Marima's," says Chloe. "Here she comes. Help us sing to her, Nathan."

Chloe pulls out her phone and starts playing the song "When the Saints Go Marching In," as our friend approaches her locker.

"What the…"

"Happy Birthday to you, Happy Birthday to you, Happy Birthday, dear Mariama, Happy Birthday to you!" we sing.

"This is so cool!" Mariama exclaims, blushing. "Thanks guys!"

"We got you a King cake, too," Chloe adds, holding out the package.

"Thank you. I'll put it in my locker and we can share it at lunch," Mariama says.

We watch Mariama put the King cake and a few of her books in her locker, and I start to feel jealous again. I'm glad my friend is happy, but I wish they had done something special for me when it was my birthday. It's true it was on a Saturday and I didn't invite anyone to a party, but they didn't get me anything.

"See you later, guys. I need to get to class," I say, making my way down the hall. I slip into my desk and get my books out of my backpack.

"Did you hear about Toby and Chloe?" Carly Gibson turns around and whispers. Carly and her brother Carlton are twins and love to know all the gossip in our class. "They are dating now!"

"Dating?!" I exclaim. "What do you mean?"

When Toby moved to our school a few months ago, Chloe couldn't stand him. To get her to like him, Toby pretended his brother had dyslexia like she does, which made her furious. Dyslexia is a disability Chloe has that makes it harder for her to read than other people, and she is really sensitive about it. Toby and Chloe have since made up, but I hardly thought they would be "dating," and what does dating mean anyway? We are only in the sixth grade!

"On our cell phone group chat last week, he told her that he liked her and they are supposed to be eating lunch together today," Carly says. "We made up a cute couple name for them: 'ToeChlo.'"

"ToeChlo?" I raise my eyebrow.

"You know, like Justin Bieber and Selena Gomez were called Jelena, or Brad Pitt and Angelina Jolie were called Brangelina."

"I don't believe it," I say. "Chloe, Mariama and I are eating lunch together today to celebrate Mariama's birthday."

"Well, you better pull up another chair for Toby," Carly laughs as the bell to start class rings.

I'm so angry I can hardly concentrate as Mrs. Bell, our English teacher, writes our assignment on the board. How could Chloe not tell me this? And of course, I missed out once again on what is going on with my friends because I don't have a phone. First, I was ignored on my birthday and now this. What else could go wrong today?

Chapter 6

Lunchtime Blues

By lunchtime I am extremely upset. Two other people have told me about ToeChlo, so I know it's fact and not fiction. If we're supposed to be best friends, how could Chloe keep me in the dark about something like this?

When I enter the lunchroom, Chloe waves me over to our usual table. My stomach drops as I spot Toby sitting beside her.

"I'm so glad that Mariama liked her birthday surprise, aren't you?" she greets me with a smile.

"What are you doing here?" I ask Toby, ignoring my friend. "I thought you liked to sit at the boys' table with the basketball team?"

"Chloe invited me to help celebrate Mari's birthday," Toby answers, stretching his arms out. "I didn't know we had assigned seats."

"Is there anything you two want to tell me?" I ask. They look at each other.

Mariama rushes up and interrupts the conversation.

"Hey guys! Let's cut some of my birthday cake."

Nathan Jones, Carlton Gibson and a couple other kids come to our table when the King cake comes out, so I stop asking questions. However, it's clear by how Chloe and Toby are acting that something is up. She laughs at all Toby's jokes and doesn't seem to mind sitting next to him, which has never happened before. He seems as comfortable as a hamburger with an order of fries by her side. I thought I was over my crush on Toby now that we had started to become friends, but now I'm not so sure. Pangs of jealousy sprout up again when I see Chloe snapping a birthday selfie with Mariama. "Let's post this on our SnapShot page," she says. "Come on, Sophie."

I bow out. Why take a picture when I don't have a cell phone to see it with?

All my friends seem to be getting closer to each other, and I feel left out.

"Aren't you going to eat your cake, Sophie?" Nathan Jones moves his chair beside mine.

He is a nice kid, but sometimes he can be a pest. I considered him my enemy when I competed against him in the spelling bee last year, but we later became friends after we stood up to a class bully together.

"I'm not really hungry," I say. "You can have it if you want."

"Thanks!" He bites off a chunk, and then pulls it out of his mouth. "There's something plastic in here."

"It's the baby!" Chloe exclaims. "Every King cake has a plastic baby in it. The person who gets it will have good luck."

"Maybe I did better on my English test than I thought I did," Nathan laughs. "I felt like I didn't know any of the answers."

"That was a hard test," Mariama agrees. "I wish I had Mrs. Bell this year. Everyone says she is a much nicer teacher."

"Yeah, Mr. Brownlee is a nightmare." Nathan turns his chair toward her and they start complaining about their English class, and completely ignore me.

Next thing you know, people will be calling them Nathiama.

Chloe and the other kids are laughing at some joke Toby is telling. I get up to put my books in my locker before my next class.

"See you later, guys."

No one seems to notices me leaving.

Chapter 7

To Tattle or Not to Tattle

The day doesn't get any better when Mom drives through the afterschool carpool line to pick me up. "We need to stop by Dad's office on the way home because I forgot to give him a patient chart he needs," she announces.

"Why couldn't you do it before you came to pick us up?" I complain. "I have lots of homework tonight."

Cole grumbles about not having his video games as soon as he slides into the backseat beside me.

"You said that I could start with the Lent stuff on Wednesday," he pouts.

"Enough with the grumbling, kids," says Mom. "Sophie, you can work on some of your assignments in the car, and you'll probably have half of them done before we get home. Cole, get a book and read it, and forget about your video games for a while."

I open up my English book and start in on some of my reading assignment. By the time we make it to Dad's office, I am almost finished with the chapter.

"Come with me into the waiting room and I will be back in just a minute." Mom grabs a file folder and makes her way to Dad's office.

Before we leave the car, Cole pulls an iPad electronic tablet from under his seat and slides it in his backpack.

"Where'd you get that?" I whisper.

"We are using them in our technology class at school," he answers.

"You know you are not supposed to be playing video games!" I say. "I'm telling Mom!"

"You're supposed to be giving up tattling for Lent," he retorts. "This is my school work and my teacher told me I could use it."

I finish up my English homework and start in on Texas history while we wait for Mom to come back.

When Cole sees her opening the door to the office, he slides the iPad back into his bag. I want to tell Mom, but feel like she will think I am tattling again if I do. I guess it's okay if Cole has to use the iPad for school, and he's done with it now anyway.

I have another hour's worth of homework once I get home from school. They weren't kidding when they said that sixth grade was a big jump up from fifth. Once I finish, I head downstairs to watch some TV before dinner is done. The spicy smell of chili hits my nose as I make my way downstairs.

"When will dinner be done?" I call into the kitchen.

"In about five minutes," Mom answers.

When I go into the family room, I see Cole at it with his video games again. This time he is playing a Video Rangers app on the laptop. Mom probably didn't notice what he was doing while she was cooking. He usually pretends he is studying using a Quizlet studying website, but I know better.

"Get off the computer, Pipsqueak," I say, snatching it from his hands. "I need to check my email."

"Mommy, Sophie is bothering me," he squeals.

"It's almost time for dinner, so why don't you two come help set the table," Mom interrupts.

Dad had to stay at the office later than usual today, so we start eating without him. My mouth feels on fire eating Mom's hot chili; she always makes it extra spicy.

"Anything interesting happen at school today?" she asks.

"Just the same old, same old," I reply.

"My teacher was talking about the Spring Spectacular," says Cole. "They are going to have a pie throwing competition and she is going to be a target."

"That I'd like to see," Mom laughs.

The garage door goes up and we hear my father's key in the lock.

"Daddy!" I yell, jumping up from the table.

"Sit down before you knock something over, young lady," Mom corrects me.

"I'm finished," Cole says, heading over to the family room and turning the laptop back on.

"What's going on here, Son?" asks Dad as he sets his files on the counter. "Finishing up homework?"

"More like finishing video game work," I reply.

"I thought we told you to try to give those games up for Lent," says Dad. "Let's put that up now."

"Can I be excused to get ready for bed?" asks Cole. "I'm tired."

Mom and Dad look at each other as Cole rushes out of the room. A few minutes later, we hear bathwater running.

"That's the first time I've heard him offer to turn in early," says Mom. "It's only 7:00 p.m."

"Well, he won't be sneaking up to play his video games, because I've put those up for a while," Dad shares.

I tell Dad and Mom about Mariama's birthday while he eats.

"They got her a huge cake, but when it was my birthday, my friends didn't think to buy me anything."

"I'm sure they didn't mean to leave you out, Sophie," says Mom. "If I remember correctly, Chloe was out of school for several days with the flu around the time of your birthday."

"Yeah, I guess, so," I agree.

After dinner, I help Mom clean the kitchen. I pass by Cole's room on the way to take my bath. He's hunched over in his bed and I yank the covers off. He scurries back like a roach hit with a flashlight.

"What the…"

"Get out of my room!" he yells.

Cole has been hiding under the covers playing his iPad. I wonder if I should tell my parents, or if they will get mad that I'm tattling again. Is it so bad that he plays games all the time? I'm not sure what to do.

Chapter 8

Bertram

I decide not to rat out my brother and head to my room for bedtime. I guess my parents will catch him when they go to tuck him in.

If I have kids when I'm older, I know one thing for sure. They will *not* be playing video games day and night. Cole is getting kind of crazy. When I think about it, a lot of other kids I go to school with play video games or check social media apps on their phones every spare moment, too.

Mom stops by to tuck me in before I drift off to sleep.

"Dad and I have a meeting with one of the workers from his office tomorrow afternoon, so I asked Mrs. Asante, Marima's mom, if you could go over there after school," she says after giving me a kiss on the cheek.

"Yay!" I pop up from the bed.

"I thought you'd like that," she smiles. "You need to keep an eye on Cole and make sure he behaves."

"He's going, too?!" I moan. "Awww man!"

"That's not nice, Sophie," Mom gently scolds. "You should be happy to watch out for your baby brother."

"He's not the innocent little baby you think he is, Mom," I whine. "When I was his age you didn't have to have anyone looking out after me. He'll just act up and keep Mariama and me from having fun."

"You can't remember what you were doing when you were Cole's age," Mom smiles. "And you won't be there that long, just for about an hour or so, so you won't have too much time for playing anyway. You will need to be getting your homework done."

"Yes ma'am," I say quietly.

She gives me a hug and moves down the hall to Cole's room.

I don't hear her fussing, so I guess he put his tablet up before she got there.

The next school day rolls by. I am so excited that I will be going home with Mariama. We've hung out at my house a few times, but I've never been to her house before.

The Asantes live only about six blocks from our school, and Mariama walks to school most days. The final school bell rings, and Mariama and I get our books from our lockers. Once Cole joins us in the school entryway, we head down the street. Though Xavier is in the Houston city limits, it's located in a neighborhood. Butterflies flit through the tree-lined streets, hot pink azalea flowers sway in bushes, and the scent of honeysuckle sweetens the breeze as we make our way to the Asante's house.

As usual, Cole is being a pest. At least two times he's bumped into my shoulder with his heavy book bag. When he slams into my back, I snap.

"If you don't get off me, boy…" I turn around and frown as he hops over a sidewalk crack.

"Oh, leave him alone, Sophie," says Mariama, smiling. "He's so cute. It must be fun to have a little brother."

"Yeah right," I grumble. "You just say that because you don't have any brothers and sisters around to annoy you."

"You're the one who's annoying." Cole sticks his tongue out at me.

Out of the corner of my eye, I see a black shape approaching.

"Look!" Cole points. "It's a dog."

Large, black eyes surrounded by curly black fur stare from the face of the animal. A white portion of fur on his chest and a black patch near his neck makes him look like he is wearing a dress shirt and bow tie. He comes up to my knees, and his mouth droops down like he's sad.

"Mmmm, mmmm, mmmm," the canine whines.

"He's wagging his tail," Cole exclaims. "That means he wants to play."

My brother reaches out and strokes the dog's head.

"Stop, Cole! It might bite you!" I exclaim.

"Ruff, ruff, ruff," barks the dog, excitedly running around Cole.

My heart beats fast in my chest and I wonder what to do. The only pet we have is my goldfish, Goldy, because my mother is allergic to fur. I don't know how to act around dogs.

Mariama starts walking faster. She's unsure around stray dogs, too.

"Let's get out of here," she says.

We move quickly down the street with the dog at our heels, tongue hanging out.

"I know how to get rid him." Cole picks up a stick and throws it down a side street.

Fast as lighting, the dog heads after it.

"Go!" shouts Mariama, and we hitch up our backpacks and hightail it around the corner.

"We lost him," I grin.

Cole whistles loudly.

"What are you doing, Silly!" I hiss.

The panting dog catches up with us again and presents Cole with the stick, its jowls turned up in a grin, then holds out his paw to shake Cole's hand.

"I just wanted to see if he could hear us," says my brother, petting his new friend again.

"Well, he'll be hearing the door shut soon, because there is my house," says Mariama, pointing to a red, brick, two-story to the right of us.

"Shoo, puppy. Go home." I point down the street as we walk up the pathway to the Asante's, but the dog refuses to budge.

"I wonder what his name is," Cole says, looking sorry for the pup.

"There's a tag around his neck, but I don't see anything written on it," Mariama says, glancing down at the dog after pressing the doorbell.

"He looks fancy," says Cole, "and he's so polite. I think I'll call him Bertram after that butler on the Disney Channel show 'Jessie.'"

"You are crazy, boy!" Mariama and I laugh.

"Welcome home," Mrs. Asante says as she opens the door and hugs her daughter, "Who do we have here?" she glances at Bertram.

"Thank you for having us, Mrs. Asante," I reply, remembering my manners. "This dog followed us home, but we don't know where he came from."

Living up to his name, Bertram holds out his paw. Mrs. Asante glances at his collar.

"Well, I see he has tags on, so he must belong to someone who lives nearby, but I don't see any names or addresses on it. He looks clean and well kept. Come in, and let's get you guys an afterschool snack. I'll call my neighbor who works with the veterinarian's office to come look at him. Sometimes dogs and cats have special chips put in them that they use to find their owners if they get lost."

"Can we give Bertram something to eat?" asks Cole.

"That's the name he gave the dog," I explain when Mrs. Asante looks at us questioningly.

"It's better not to feed him, or he'll never go away," she said. "Let's get you guys inside for a snack."

Bertram looks up with puppy dog eyes as we close the door.

Chapter 9

The Asantes

We set our backpacks by the entrance and follow Mariama into the living area.

Sky blue walls filled with colorful African paintings and masks decorate the room. On the mantle over the fireplace sits a large photograph of Mariama and her parents wearing traditional African clothing. Last year, Mariama, Chloe and I wore African gowns and head wraps that her mom made us for our school's twin day, which was really neat.

"Wow, this is so cool!" Cole exclaims, moving to touch a floor statue of an elephant.

"Leave that alone!" I smack his hand.

A tangy, spicy scent hits my nose as we enter the kitchen, and my stomach starts grumbling. There's a plate filled with pastries on the table.

"Yum! Can we have some of those desserts?" asks Cole as I nudge him to be quiet.

"Help yourself," smiles Mrs. Asante, "but they are not desserts; they are meat pies."

"I've never had meat in a pie before," says Cole, picking one up and taking a bite. "Ummm, this is pretty good."

"They are delicious. Thank you, Mrs. Asante," I say, helping myself to a couple.

"Want some juice?" asks Mariama. "We nod our heads yes, and sit down at the table.

"Thank you guys again for my birthday surprise," says Mariama, pouring our drinks. "I wasn't expecting it at all."

"I'm glad you liked it," I say, feeling guilty because I had been jealous when Chloe came up with the idea.

After we finish eating, Mariama gets out her notebook, and following her cue, Cole and I settle down to do our homework at the kitchen table. About 40 minutes later, we finish. Mariama gets out a card game called Uno and we deal the cards to play.

"Uno!" I shout, stopping Cole from beating us. He laughs and gives me five rather than whining as he does when he loses at home.

It's fun spending time with my good friend, and even my little brother is behaving for once.

Ding dong!

The front doorbell rings.

"Awww man! Not Mom already." Cole exclaims.

The door squeaks open and I hear her voice. "Thanks so much for allowing the children to come over after school, Mrs. Asante. You are a lifesaver."

"No problem," Mrs. Asante replies. "Your children are very well-behaved, and Mariama enjoys the company."

Our parents walk into the kitchen.

"Can they stay a while longer?" Mariama begs.

"Sorry Sweetie, but we need to get home for dinner; it's a school night," Mom shakes her head. "Maybe they can come over again on a Friday, or a weekend, or we can have you over to our house."

"Mmmmm ... Mmmmm ... Mmmmm," ... scratch, scratch, scratch.

Mariama peeks out the back door.

"That dog is still out there, Mom."

"Hey Bertram," Cole coos.

An older woman with red-rimmed glasses approaches from behind the dog.

"Hello, Mrs. McVee," greets Mrs. Asante.

"After you called me, I had to come over to see your new guests," Mrs. McVee says, stroking Bertram's head.

"These are our friends, Mrs. Washington and her children, Sophie and Cole," introduces Mrs. Asante.

"Nice to meet you," Mrs. McVee replies. She examines Bertram's tag. "This dog definitely belongs to someone. He looks like an expensive breed, a Portuguese Water Dog."

"We named him Bertram," pipes up Cole.

"Get back, Mom," I caution. "He might make you sneeze."

My mother is allergic to animal fur, and that is why my parents have never let my brother and me get any pets besides our fish.

"No need to worry about this one if you have allergies," says Mrs. McVee. "Portuguese Water Dogs are hypoallergenic, so he shouldn't make you sneeze or cough."

"Maybe we can keep him, Mom!" suggests Cole.

"I don't know about that. I'm sure his owners are wondering where he is."

"Ewww! What's that?" Mariama points at a brown pile behind the dog.

"Looks like Bertram is making himself at home," snickers Mrs. McVee.

"Well, that answers any questions in my mind about him staying here," Mrs. Asante says, wrinkling her nose in disgust. "Absolutely not."

"Don't worry about me asking to keep him, Mom," agrees Mariama. "Making my bed every day and helping wash the dishes are enough. I don't want to have to clean up after a dog."

"I wouldn't mind," counters Cole.

"I'll get the vet to look at his chip and see where he comes from," Mrs. McVee says as she scoops up the mess and puts it in a plastic bag, then

SOPHIE WASHINGTON: THE GAMER

attaches a lease to Bertram's collar. "Then we'll let you know where he belongs."

She walks across to her backyard, and Mom steers me and Cole toward the front of the house.

"Thank you again, Mrs. Asante. See you later."

Chapter 10

Go Rockets

When we got home from school on Friday, our parents had a special treat.

"Dad got tickets for the Rockets game to-night," says Mom.

"Yay!" Cole and I high-five each other. It's the first time I've seen him smile this wide since his video games were locked up on Wednesday. Though our rescue of Bertram cheered him up somewhat, he was still grumbling about not being able to play. At school, Mariama said they hadn't heard back from Mrs. McVee about Bertram's owners yet.

We love to go see live Houston Rockets basketball. Our parents get tickets to at least two games a year. I don't like watching sports on television, but it's so much fun to feel the excitement of the crowd in Toyota Stadium. The Rocket's mascot, Clutch the Bear, always cracks me up with his crazy pranks and stunts, and Mom and Dad let us get our favorite snacks at the game.

Cole has played basketball on youth teams for the past two years and knows the names of all the professional basketball players. He thinks he's good enough to join the NBA now.

"We'll be leaving in about 40 minutes, so let's get ready," says Dad.

Cole runs upstairs to change out of his school uniform into his Rockets basketball jersey, and I put on my red Rockets t-shirt. I decide to wear my red Converse high-top sneakers to match the outfit. When we get downstairs, Mom and Dad are wearing red shirts, too.

As soon as we walk into the arena I smell hot buttered popcorn and sweet cotton candy.

"Can we get snacks, Mom?" I ask.

The crowd at the stadium matches us all with their red jerseys, t-shirts and caps. We head to the concession stand, and Cole and I order hotdogs, chips and sodas. Mom and Dad make us get healthy food most of the time, so this is a real treat.

"You can buy some other snacks at halftime," says Dad as we make our way to our seats. We are in a middle section that is not too far up from the court.

I watch the players warm up on the floor, throwing up practice layups and free-throw shots.

"It looks like they never miss," I say.

"That's why they are pros," Cole replies.

"Goooo Rockets!!!" yells the announcer over the sound system.

The Rockets Power Dancers bounce to the floor and pull out slingshots.

"What are they doing?" asks Cole.

Hundreds of t-shirts fling up in the stands in response.

"I caught one!" My brother hugs the red Rockets t-shirt close.

"Great catch, Son!" Dad pats him on the back.

I try to get a t-shirt, but no more come in our direction.

Braaaaaaaaah! A horn sounds and the game begins.

The play gets intense as the Rockets trade baskets back and forth with their opponents. The lead player hits a buzzer beater, three-point shot at halftime, and we jump out of our seats yelling.

The players go to their locker room for the break, and Clutch the Mascot bear runs toward our section.

"Hey, over here, Clutch!" I yell.

He heads near our seats!

"Quick, Mom, let's get a selfie," I shout. She pulls out her cell phone.

The huge furry bear poses for a picture with me and I'm all smiles.

"That's so cool!" enthuses Cole, checking out the photo.

We get cotton candy to enjoy at the end of the game. Cole and Dad pump their fists in the air when one of the Rockets makes a slam dunk. Sadly, they are down by five points when the final buzzer sounds to signal the game is over, but we had a great time.

"Thanks, Mom and Dad, for taking us to the game," says Cole.

"We had so much fun," I add.

"I'm happy we could enjoy the game together." Dad puts his arm around me.

On our way back to our car, we see a homeless man beating a tune on an upside down bucket with a tin can for money at his feet. Dad slides a few dollars in his can and I feel blessed that we are able to enjoy this night.

Chapter 11

Bertram Washington

"Guess what?"

Mariama is so excited she doesn't pause to say hello after I answer the phone.

"Bertram's owners are looking for a new home for him, and my mom asked if you all want him."

"What?!" I exclaim in surprise. Last year I begged my parents for a dog, but I had pretty much given up on the idea when they told me my mom has bad allergies and furry animals make her sick. I never realized there was such thing as a hypoallergenic dog until Mrs. McVee told us.

"You sure *you* don't want Bertram?" I ask.

"Nah, I don't really like dogs, and my mother doesn't want to clean up after it. Mrs. McVee said the owners just had a new baby and don't have time to take care of a dog. They are trying to find it a new home. And they call him Fluffy, by the way."

"Let me ask my parents and call you back." I hang up the phone and look for my parents.

They are in the family room watching television. Cole is sitting on the couch between them, moping.

"Why don't you go play something, Sweetie?" Mom nudges him with her elbow.

"There's nothing to do," he whines. "You locked up all my games, and I don't have anything else to play that's not boring."

"This is ridiculous," says Dad. "You have an electric scooter, a basketball goal in the driveway, at least 20 dress-up costumes, art supplies, and more books and board games than I can count. Plus, it's a beautiful, sunny day. Go outside and find some other kids to play with."

"When I was your age, we used our imaginations," Mom chimes in.

"They are probably in their houses playing video games, Dad," Cole pouts. "It's what kids do in modern times."

I interrupt the discussion.

"Mariama just called me and asked if we want Bertram."

"Really?" Cole jumps up and happily pumps his fist in the air.

"Who is Bertram?" asks Dad.

"That stray dog that followed the kids home from the Asante's," says Mom.

"Please, please, please, Mom and Dad?" Cole begs. "I really want a dog. I'll help take care of him, and he's hyper-genic so he won't make Mom sick."

"It's hypoallergenic, Silly," I correct him.

"I've never really wanted a pet because of your mom's allergies," says Dad thoughtfully, "but if he's hypoallergenic, this could be another way to teach you kids responsibility, and get you outside more and away from the video games."

"Does this mean we can have him, Dad?!!" I ask excitedly.

"Let's call the Asantes and get more information," says Mom.

While she goes to talk on the phone, Cole and I google Portuguese Water Dogs on the Internet to find out more information on taking care of Bertram.

"This says that Portuguese Water Dogs need lots of exercise, so I will give him a walk every day," says Cole, scrolling through the article I pull up.

"It also says they are great family dogs. We will tell that to Mom and Dad if they have any arguments about us getting him," I add.

An hour later it was official. Bertram was coming to live with us.

"We hadn't planned on getting a dog, but we think you kids will benefit," Dad explains.

"Let's get some supplies at the pet store, and we can pick him up from the Asante's tomorrow morning," Mom adds.

Cole and I are so excited we can't stop smiling. I can't believe we are getting our very own dog. We clear out an area in the laundry room to put

Bertram's bed, water and food bowls. Later, Cole makes a banner to hang over the door for our new pet's arrival: "Welcome Home Bertram Washington."

Chapter 12

Dog Eat Dog

Once we get Bertram home, life in our house gets busier. He is very active, and definitely encourages us to go outside more.

"Mmmmm. Mmmmm. Mmmmm."

Bertram stands at the door, leash under his paws, every time we come home from school, begging for his afternoon walk. Sometimes Cole and Dad take him for an extra stroll around the block after dinner before the sun goes down.

Mom won't admit it, but she likes having the dog around, too. I see her sneaking Bertram extra doggy treats when no one's looking.

I've gotten over my fear of touching Bertram, and love to see him get happy after I scratch his back or rub his belly. In spite of the accident he had on the Asante's back patio, Bertram was house trained by his prior owners, so he lets us know when he needs to go outside by scratching near the door.

Cole has been so busy with our new pet that he hasn't had time to worry about his locked-up video games and has stopped complaining about them completely.

"Thanks so much, Mom and Dad, for letting us get a dog," he says, pouring food into Bertram's bowl.

While I'm doing my homework, Bertram likes to lie at the foot of my bed. I keep a careful eye on him whenever he's in my room, because when we did our Google research I read that Portuguese Water Dogs like to eat fish, and he's been eyeballing my goldfish Goldy since day one.

"You stick to your dog food, Bertram," I say, moving Goldy to the highest shelf on my bookcase. Dad got Goldy for me last year as a surprise gift after I won the school spelling bee. Back then, I would have never believed that we'd have a family dog just a year later.

Bertram fits into our family as smoothly as peanut butter with jelly, I think, happily stroking his soft, furry head.

"Has anyone seen my black shoe?" I hear Dad calling from downstairs. "I only see one of them in the downstairs closet."

"Check in the laundry room, Dear," Mom instructs from the kitchen. "You left them there yesterday."

"Sophie! Cole! Downstairs! And bring the dog with you!" Dad thunders a few minutes later.

"Come on, boy." I coax Bertram down the steps with me and see Cole making his way to the laundry room from the kitchen.

Wonder what's up?

Bertram cocks his head to the side as we enter the laundry room. We all stop at the doorway when we see my father's scowling face. He is holding his chewed-up new shoe in his hand.

"The condition of you kids getting your dog was that you take care of him," Dad says. "Now who can explain how Bertram got ahold of my shoe?"

"I read on the Internet that dogs like to chew things," I say. "Maybe we should get Bertram some bones or toys to chew on."

"Sorry about your shoe, Dad," says Cole. "We'll keep a better eye on what Bertram is doing."

"And we should all keep our shoes in the closet and not on the laundry room floor where the dog sleeps from now on," says Mom, kissing Dad's cheek. "Why don't you wear your brown shoes today?"

Later that afternoon, we get another surprise. "Look at my change purse!!!" Mom holds up a chewed-up wad. "I've been looking for this since yesterday!"

"Guess I'm not the only one who should put my things up," jokes Dad with a wink. "We may need to get Mr. Bertram some dog training."

"Or maybe we should be feeding him more," jokes Cole.

That evening, Cole storms into my room, flaming mad. "Just look what Bertram did!" he wails, holding up a joystick chewed down to the wire. Bertram cowers behind my bed. "Now I won't be able to play my games when I get them back!"

"What's all the racket up here?" Mom steps in.

"Bertram took a bite out of Cole's video game controller," I giggle.

"I wouldn't laugh too much," Cole says. "Next time he may chew up something of yours."

"Yeah," I laugh, "now when I hear people say their dog ate their homework at school, I'll know they are telling the truth."

Chapter 13

Spring Spectacular

"Hurry up, Sophie! Dad and I are getting in the car and leaving in less than five minutes!" Cole yells up to me as he and my father open the back door to the garage. I take one last glance in the mirror, grab my favorite tennis shoes, pat Bertram on the head, and rush behind them.

The day of our school's Spring Spectacular festival is finally here, and I can't wait to get there. Xavier Academy hosts the special fundraiser two weeks before Easter each spring, rain or shine. If the weather is bad, festivities take place in the gym. Outside or in, it's lots of fun, and my friends and I never miss it. Bouncy houses, pony rides, go carts and booths filled with games, barbecue, hot dogs, funnel cakes, candy apples, slushies and loads of other carnival goodies fill the campus. At the end of the day there is a large raffle with cool prizes like movie passes, gift cards, and even flat-screen televisions. Usually, my mother volunteers at one of the booths, but this year she's missing out because she has a book club meeting with her friends, so Dad said he would bring us.

"Sophie!" My friends, Chloe and Mariama, swarm on me like bees to honey as soon as we step on campus. "Do you have any tickets? Let's play some games! Hi Mr. Washington and Cole."

"We just got here," I explain to my friends. "We haven't bought our tickets yet."

"Okay, see you in few." Chloe and Mariama make their way to the pony rides and we line up at the ticket counter.

Cole points out a giant slide while we wait.

"Can we go on that, Daddy?"

"I don't know, Son, it looks pretty high in the air," Dad says, squinting at the ride.

"I can slide down it myself if you're too scared," Cole answers.

"We'll see, Son," Dad laughs.

While in line, Cole and I write our names on raffle tickets we had bought at school last week, and put them in a large box for the big drawing.

The sun beams down on us and I wipe sweat off my forehead. I see my friends finishing up their rides on the pony and moving toward a food booth.

"I wish they would hurry up!" I say impatiently. After what feels like forever, we finally get our game tickets. Dad gives me a pack of fifty tickets and tells me I can go with my friends.

"Meet us back here at the ticket booth at four o'clock," he says.

"Chloe, Mariama!" I call.

We have a ball jumping in the bouncy house, drinking large slushies, and getting our faces painted. I get flowers, Chloe gets butterflies, and Mariama gets a rainbow.

"Hey girls, how long have you been here?" Toby, Nathan and Carlton spot us leaving the face painting.

"My parents are picking me up in an hour, but Sophie just got here," Chloe answers, blushing at Toby.

"Want to go on the giant slide?"

"Sure," says Mariama. "Chloe and I went down it earlier and it's really fast."

I look up at the slide and my heart starts to flutter. It's so tall, it seems to reach in the clouds. I've always been afraid of heights, and I usually avoid roller coasters and rides that are way up in the air. I get ready to tell my friends I will sit this one out.

"Hey, isn't that your little brother, Sophie?" Toby interrupts me, pointing to the top of the slide. We watch as Cole scoots to the top of the slide, quickly drops, moves to his belly mid-slide and ends with a forward roll. People on the ground are actually clapping for him.

"Whoa, he's a real daredevil, isn't he?" exclaims Mariama, clasping her hands.

"I'm sure he learned his tricks from his cool big sister, eh?" Toby playfully elbows me in the ribs.

I don't see my dad anywhere around, but I'm sure he can't be happy with my little brother's stunt.

"Come on guys, let's go before the line gets long again," urges Chloe.

I follow along, reluctantly, feeling my stomach getting queasy.

"What time is it, Mariama?" I ask, trying to find a way out. "I have to meet up with my father at four."

"It's only 3:15, so we have plenty of time," she answers. "I need to go home around then, too."

We start climbing the stairs to the slide and I feel more and more nauseous. *What have I gotten myself into?* My friends zip down the slide one after another, and just Toby and I are left. "Ladies first." He steps aside to let me have a turn.

There's no turning back now. I sit down on the edge and feel another heaving in my stomach.

Then I throw up all over the slide.

Chapter 14

Raffle Ticket

"Gross!" I hear the girl behind Toby yelling. "That girl just barfed."

"Are you okay, Sophie?" Toby touches my shoulder.

I'm so embarrassed I don't know what to say.

"Everybody, make your way down the stairs!" shouts the slide operator. "Watch your step please."

Toby helps me as we climb backwards down the stairs.

To my relief, I see my father in the waiting crowd and rush to his side.

"It's alright, Sweetie." He wraps me in a bear hug.

Caution tape is put on the slide entrance so people will know it is shut down.

I feel something sticky on Dad's back.

"What the…?"

"I'll explain later," he whispers, seeing my friends running up to check on me.

"We're sorry, Sophie," say Chloe and Mariama, rushing over to us.

"Why didn't you tell us you were feeling sick?"

"I didn't know until I got to the top of the slide," I say.

"I see my mom over there, coming to pick me up," says Mariama. "She's dropping Chloe off at her house."

"Okay, see you at school tomorrow," I respond.

The boys from my class scatter, and I follow beside my father and Cole.

"I thought people would remember my slide over everyone's today," said my little brother, "but you've got me topped. Did you see how that throw up gushed out of her mouth, Dad?"

"That's enough, Son," my father cuts him off. "We've had more than our share of excitement for the day. It's time to head home."

"Guess what happened to Daddy right after you left us, Sophie?" Cole shares. "He got hit in the face with a pie."

"How did that happen?" I cover my mouth with my hand to stifle a giggle.

"Cole wanted to try out the 'Pie Your Teacher Booth,' and the elementary school principal asked me to give them a hand while she pulled out some more desserts from the cooler," Dad explains.

"One of the kids thought Dad was that fourth-grade teacher, Mr. Mitchell, and threw a pie at him when he turned around," Cole bursts in. "It was hilarious!"

"I'm just happy he only got my face and not my clothes, or you guys would have had to go home early," Dad says.

We stop to buy cold bottles of water and hear an announcement being made.

"It's time for the raffle results. All those who purchased raffle tickets, please gather at booth 10."

"Sophie and I bought raffle tickets last week," says Cole. "Can we see if we won before we leave?"

Dad looks at me to see how I'm doing, and I nod my head that it's okay. I feel more embarrassed about what happened than sick. I'm glad my friends were so nice to me and didn't laugh, and I'm happy I didn't throw up on anyone else.

We make our way to booth 10, and Cole and I pull out our raffle tickets.

The crowd around the booth isn't as large as I expected it would be, but since tomorrow is a school day, some people have already gone home. It doesn't look like anyone recognizes me from the slide or Dad from the pie booth, because no one is looking at us funny.

"The first ticket is 8873," reads the announcer, "and the prize is two movie tickets, and a voucher for popcorn and drinks."

A lady in the crowd runs up and shows her ticket.

Three other ticket numbers are read and none of them are ours. Finally, the last prize is announced. "We have a brand new, PlayStation video game system up for grabs to the owner of ticket number 6753."

"That's me!" shouts Cole, jumping up and down. "I have the winning ticket!!"

"That's great, Son," says Dad, taking him up to collect his prize.

This is unbelievable. Now Cole has three video game systems that he isn't allowed to play, and I have not one cell phone.

"Will I be able to play it?" Cole asks as we make our way back to the car with the new PlayStation.

"Not until after Lent, Son," Dad replies.

"But that's two weeks from now. It's not fair!" pouts Cole, "and you and Mom forced me to give up video games for Lent. I didn't want to."

"Two weeks is no time at all, Cole," says Dad. "There will still be limits on the games if we let you play, because your mom and I feel like all this gaming is getting out of control."

"How long will I get to play it?" Cole whines.

"Your mother and I will discuss it when we get home," Dad answers. "We will have some guidelines set around how much you can play when we give the games back after Lent."

Chapter 15

Overdue iPad

Mom laughs when we relay the Spring Spectacular happenings.

"Looks like I missed an eventful day. The most exciting thing that happened in our book club was that Mrs. Simpson dropped her chip in the salsa."

"I don't know why you think it's funny that I got sick on the slide," I pout.

"Or that I won a game I can't play," Cole frowns.

"You're both right, and I'm happy you two are okay." Mom gives us hugs.

"What about me?" Dad fake cries. "I had to suffer with pie in my face and sick children all day, all by my lonesome."

"I'm glad you're alright too, Sweetie," Mom pecks his cheek. "Yum, you taste like lemon meringue."

"Can you guys stop?!" I smile with embarrassment.

"Ruff! Ruff!" barks Bertram.

That night, I hear Cole banging around in his room. When I get to the door, I see him frantically searching through his toy box. Next, he pulls the mattress off his bed.

"Looking for something?" I ask.

"I can't find my iPad, and it is due back at school on Friday," he says.

"I thought they let you bring that home for a project," I say.

"It's just for a certain period of time from the library," he answers. "They say I have to pay a $200 fee if I don't turn it in tomorrow."

"I wondered why they let second graders take something that expensive home."

"You had to have your parents sign a permission slip for you to bring one home," he says, eyes wide.

"You mean you copied Mom and Dad's signatures on the permission slip to get an iPad?" I clarify.

Cole sadly shakes his head yes. *I guess he's been using his great drawing skills for something lately after all, faking Mom and Dad's signatures!*

"You'd better find that iPad, or you are in big trouble!" I start helping him look around the room. "Did you leave it downstairs?"

"The last time I had it was up here, Thursday night, before I went to bed," he sighs.

I feel bad for my brother, because I wonder if he learned some of this sneakiness from me. Last year, when my parents wouldn't buy me a cell phone, I secretly convinced one of Cole's friends to lend me his, then got it taken away when I had it out in class.

I think of something.

"When was the last time Bertram was in your room, Cole?"

"I played with him some Thursday night..." he responds thoughtfully. "Maybe he has my iPad!"

Chapter 16

Chew Toy

We rush to the laundry room, and I pray on the way that my suspicions aren't true. We still hadn't had time to buy Bertram any chew toys after he destroyed Dad's shoe and Mom's wallet, so he may have been searching for something else to gnaw on.

"Bertram, here boy," I call.

He is sleeping in his dog bed and lifts his head up questioningly at my voice.

"Do you have my iPad?" Cole asks. "Where is it?"

Cole moves to lift the dog up out of its bed.

"What's going on here?" Mom comes to the laundry room door. "Shouldn't you kids be getting ready for bed?"

"I'm missing one of my toys, and I'm seeing if Bertram has it," Cole answers.

Bertram hops up out of the dog bed. Underneath him is the iPad.

"There it is!" Cole exclaims. "It's like he was laying an egg or something."

He picks up the iPad to examine it, so excited he forgets Mom is there.

"Where did you get an iPad, young man?"

"From school," he answers.

"I thought those had to be checked out with parental permission, and we agreed not to get you one this term to avoid you being tempted to play video games," she frowns.

I see Cole struggling to make up a tale to tell Mom and step in. "He copied your name on the permission slip so he could check out an iPad."

"Cole!" Mom looks at him in surprise.

"Thanks for snitching on me, Rat," my brother scowls. "I guess you gave up on your Lent promise to quit tattling all the time."

"I just feel bad, Cole," I explain. "You've been lying to Mom and Dad all this time, and I don't want you to get into any more trouble. If Bertram had broken your iPad, we'd have to pay for it."

"That's right, young man," Mom scolds. "Your sister is doing you a favor by making you tell the truth. Piling untruth upon untruth just lands you into deeper trouble."

"Take it from me, bro, that's something you do *not* want," I add, remembering a time earlier in the school year when I lied to my friends and parents to become more popular, and got into one mishap after another.

Mom makes sure that the iPad is working properly, and then puts it in Cole's backpack.

"Head up to your room, Squirt. I need to talk with your father later about how we will deal with this."

She turns to me after my brother has left the room.

"I'm proud of how you handled yourself, Sophie. I'm sure you didn't want to turn in your little brother, but you did the right thing. I know your father and I have fussed at you in the past for tattling so much, but you really used good judgment here and helped keep Cole out of trouble."

"Thanks Mom," I say, giving her a hug before going to wash up for bed. I peep into Cole's room again and he scowls at me.

Being a big sister is tough sometimes, but I'm happy I helped my little brother. I know from experience that honesty is the best policy. Hopefully, he'll thank me later.

Chapter 17

Rodeo Artist

Cole is still angry with me at breakfast the next morning.

"Pass the syrup, traitor."

But the chip on his shoulder has fallen off by the time Mom picks us up after school that day.

"Guess what?" he buzzes as we both slide in the car. "My painting was picked for the state rodeo art contest!"

"That's awesome, Cole," I say with a smile.

"For the second year in a row! Wonderful!" echoes Mom.

"Here's the sheet my teacher gave me." He passes it up to Mom.

"She says your painting is exceptional for a student your age, and she's extremely proud of you," my mother beams.

"I've been working on it extra in after care, since my games were taken away and I had nothing else to do," Cole says sheepishly.

"Well, I'm happy to see you have been making good use of your time," Mom says, winking through the rearview mirror as we pull out of the school parking lot.

We stop off for slushies on the way home to celebrate.

"What is your painting of?" I ask.

"We had to paint scenery from Texas, so I did a painting of a cowboy riding a bull," he describes.

"I can't wait to see it," says Mom.

"We'll get it back once they send it off for judging," Cole replies.

"If I remember correctly from last year, so that should be in about two weeks," Mom adds.

When we get home, Cole goes to work organizing Dad's tools in the garage, his punishment for sneaking the school iPad home.

I grab a popsicle from the freezer and take Bertram down the street for a walk.

"Hey Sophie, is Cole home?" Our neighbor Jake approaches on his scooter. Jake is in second grade like Cole, and shows up anytime we are outside with a snack.

As if on cue, he eyes my treat and asks, "Do you all have any more of those strawberry popsicles?"

"Sorry Jake, this is the last one. And Cole has to do some work so he can't play today."

"Okay, tell him I said hi," he responds, zooming off down the street.

"Ruff, ruff," Bertram barks after him.

An hour later, the dog and I return home. Cole is at the kitchen table drawing.

"At it again?" I ask.

"Just something I've been working on," he says.

The drawing is of our entire family, and includes Bertram sitting at our feet.

"It's adorable, Cole! Wait until Mom and Dad see this!"

"Thanks Sophie. Sorry I've been so mean to you lately," says Cole.

"Don't worry about it, Squirt," I say, patting his head. "That's what little brothers are for."

Chapter 18

Easter Sunday

The day Cole has been a waiting for weeks has finally arrived, Easter Sunday! The sun is shining bright outside, and we find cute Easter baskets filled with jelly beans, candy marshmallows, chocolate bunnies and colored eggs near our places at the breakfast table. After eating and cleaning up the kitchen, we dress to get ready for church.

Surprisingly, Cole hasn't mentioned getting his video games back, and my parents haven't said anything about it either.

I slip on the pretty white Easter dress Mom and I picked out at the mall this weekend, and gather up my white lace Easter gloves and special hair bows. Dad and Cole look very handsome in matching, tan-colored suits, yellow shirts and bow ties, and Mom is wearing a fitted white dress, heels and a fancy church hat.

"I wish we had someone to take a family picture of us," she says. "It's been awhile since we've all been dressed up like this."

"Maybe we can get another family to take a shot of us after church," Dad suggests.

The church is filled with scented white lily flowers, and the choir's sweet singing swells through the crowd. Our pastor gives a stirring sermon about how Jesus died on the cross for our sins. Cole and I only nod off once, and Mom slips us peppermint candies to keep us alert.

"Hi Chloe!" I wave to my friend and her family as they make their way towards us after church.

"Happy Easter!" Mr. Hopkins, Chloe's father, shakes my dad's hand. "Nice seeing you all."

Chloe and I admire each other's outfits and Cole pulls at his scratchy bow tie.

"I thought getting a suit would be better than wearing short pants and a vest, but no such luck," he complains.

"Well, you look very handsome, indeed," compliments Mrs. Hopkins.

The Hopkins snaps our family's picture outside the church entrance, and we take theirs for them.

"I will cherish this," says Mom, reviewing the picture on her phone.

On the drive home, Dad makes an announcement.

"Lent is officially over, and I hope that you learned something. Sophie, your mother and I have been pleased at how you have tried to count your blessings more and complain less. While we were disappointed that you fooled us, Cole, we feel like you have also gotten a better understanding of why it's important to not spend all your time playing video games."

"Thanks Dad," Cole responds. "I missed playing my games as much as I wanted to, but I am happy I finished my painting and it was picked for the art contest."

"We're going to let you play your video games again, on a more limited basis," Dad says, "but first let's have our Easter dinner."

Those are words to my ears, because I'm always starving after we return from church. As soon as we change our clothes and Mom heats things up, we feast on a delicious meal of ham, green beans, potato salad, deviled eggs and homemade rolls.

After Christmas, Easter is my favorite holiday.

Chapter 19

Game Night

That evening we host our weekly game night. Mom and Dad started game night as a time for us to gather as a family without electronics, but tonight my father says we are doing something different.

"Cole hasn't gotten a chance to use the new PlayStation game he won at the raffle, so we are going to have a family video game battle, parents against the kids."

"Are you kidding me?" Cole grins. "There is no way you can beat us at video games. Get ready to give me my respect, Dad. It's on."

I shake my head laughing. "I don't think you can beat Cole at his video games either, Daddy, and I know Mom can't."

"As a condition of playing, we get to choose the games and our opponents," says Mom, pulling out a plastic store bag. Inside is a video dance game that she challenges me to play.

"Okay, let's do this!" I say.

The game has video generated characters dancing to popular songs. Players mimic the dances, and the computer somehow tracks your movements and scores how well you do.

We get started, and Bertram rushes into the room to find out what all the commotion is about. He wags his tail happily, then sits at the foot of the couch to watch.

"I didn't know Mom could dance so well," Cole jumps up and down giggling, as our mother busts a move beside me.

Twenty minutes later, she plops down on the sofa with a smile. "I surrender."

"I beat you by just ten points, Mom, so you can hold your head high."

Dad and Cole take over the competition next, playing a football video game that Dad used to love that is still updated each year.

"I've been winning this game since before you were born, Son," he teases Cole as he gains yardage.

Both of their teams score touchdowns, and we break to eat some of Mom's strawberry shortcake.

"This is the best Easter holiday ever!" Cole exclaims.

"I'm happy that we've found a way to include the things you kids like with our time together as a family," says Mom, "but remember, we won't be playing video games day and night just because they are out again."

"Yes ma'am," agrees Cole.

The game continues for another half hour, and Mom and I pretend to be cheerleaders for each side, me for Dad and her for Cole.

"Two, four, six, eight, who do we appreciate? Cole, Cole, Goooo Cole!"

Finally, Dad prevails as the winner.

"I can't believe he beat me," Cole grins and shakes his head in shock. "If my friends hear about this, I'll be too embarrassed."

"Don't hate the player, Son," laughs Dad, patting his back. "Hate the game."

Chapter 20

Morning After

I sleep in the next morning because we have the school day off. Mom wakes me up by gently touching my forehead.

"Wake up, Princess. You don't want to dream the day away."

"Huh? Oh, good morning, Mom," I mumble, squinting my eyes.

I see a shiny gold package in her hand and sit up.

"What's that?"

"Just a little gift from your father and me," my mother smiles.

I rip off the wrapping paper and blink at what's inside.

"A cell phone! Thanks so much, Mom!"

I lean in to give her a big hug.

"You've been showing more maturity lately, and we think you're ready for your own phone," says Mom. "We also feel it's only fair you have a cell phone, since your brother got a new game system. He'll be allowed to play it on weekends, for no more than four hours, and we will have some limits on your cell phone use as well. With me working with your dad at his office more, we expect you to use the phone responsibly to keep up with us after school as well."

"I'll take really good care of it," I nod my head and smile.

"We're proud of you, Sweetie. Enjoy!" Mom heads back downstairs.

I'm stunned. Just when I thought I had my parents figured out, they surprise me again. If I had known ratting out Cole would have gotten me a cell phone, I would have done it sooner. It feels good to know that my parents see me as being more grown up. I can't wait to get to school tomorrow to tell all my friends.

I go to the bathroom and wash up, then get dressed in my room.

Bertram bounds through the door with his leash in his teeth begging for a walk, and I smile. I'll set up my cell phone later.

"You're right, boy. It's time to get outside for the start of another great day!"

Dear Reader:

Thank you for reading *Sophie Washington: The Gamer*! I hope you liked it. If you enjoyed the book, I'd be grateful if you post a short review on Amazon. Your feedback really makes a difference and helps others learn about my books.

I appreciate your support!

Tonya Duncan Ellis

Books by
Tonya Duncan Ellis

For information on all Tonya Duncan Ellis books about Sophie and her friends

Check out the following pages!

You'll find:

- Blurbs about the other exciting books in the Sophie Washington series

- Information about Tonya Duncan Ellis

Sophie Washington: Queen of the Bee

Sign up for the spelling bee?

No way!

If there's one thing 10-year-old Texan Sophie Washington is good at, it's spelling. She's earned straight 100s on all her spelling tests to prove it. Her parents want her to compete in the Xavier Academy spelling bee, but Sophie wishes they would buzz off.

Her life in the Houston suburbs is full of adventures, and she doesn't want to slow down the action. Where else can you chase wild hogs out of your yard, ride a bucking sheep, or spy an eight-foot-long alligator during a bike ride through the neighborhood? Studying spelling words seems as fun as getting stung by a hornet, in comparison.

That's until her irritating classmate, Nathan Jones, challenges her. There's no way she can let Mr. Know-It-All win. Studying is hard when you have a pesky younger brother and a busy social calendar. Can Sophie ignore the distractions and become Queen of the Bee?

Sophie Washington:
The Snitch

There's nothing worse than being a tattletale...

That's what 10-year-old Sophie Washington thinks until she runs into Lanie Mitchell, a new girl at school. Lanie pushes Sophie and her friends around at their lockers, and even takes their lunch money.

If they tell, they are scared the other kids in their class will call them snitches and won't be their friends. And when you're in the fifth grade, nothing seems worse than that.

Excitement at home keeps Sophie's mind off the trouble with Lanie.

She takes a fishing trip to the Gulf of Mexico with her parents and little brother, Cole, and discovers a mysterious creature in the attic above her room. For a while, Sophie is able to keep her parents from knowing what is going on at school. But Lanie's bullying goes too far, and a classmate gets seriously hurt. Sophie needs to make a decision. Should she stand up to the bully, or become a snitch?

Sophie Washington: Things You Didn't Know About Sophie

Oh, the tangled web we weave...

Sixth grader Sophie Washington thought she had life figured out when she was younger, but this school year, everything changed. She feels like an outsider because she's the only one in her class without a cell phone, and her crush, new kid Toby Johnson, has been calling her best friend Chloe. To fit in, Sophie changes who she is. Her plan to become popular works for a while, and she and Toby start to become friends.

In between the boy drama, Sophie takes a whirlwind class field trip to Austin, TX, where she visits the state museum, eats Tex-Mex food, and has a wild ride on a kayak. Back at home, Sophie fights off buzzards from her family's roof, dissects frogs in science class, and has fun at her little brother Cole's basketball tournament.

Things get more complicated when Sophie "borrows" a cell phone and gets caught. If her parents make her tell the truth, what will her friends think? Turns out Toby has also been hiding something, and Sophie discovers the best way to make true friends is to be yourself.

Sophie Washington: The Gamer

40 Days Without Video Games? Oh No!

Sixth-grader Sophie Washington and her friends are back with an interesting book about having fun with video games while keeping balance. It's almost Easter, and Sophie and her family get ready to start fasts for Lent with their church, where they give up doing something for 40 days that may not be good for them. Her parents urge Sophie to stop tattling so much and encourage her second-grade brother Cole to give up something he loves most, playing video games. The kids agree to the challenge, but how long can they keep it up? Soon after Lent begins, Cole starts sneaking to play his video games. Things start to get out of control when he loses a school electronic tablet he checked out without his parents' permission and comes to his sister for help. Should Sophie break her promise and tattle on him?

Sophie Washington: Hurricane

#Sophie Strong

A hurricane's coming, and eleven-year-old Sophie Washington's typical middle school life in the Houston, Texas suburbs is about to make a major change. One day she's teasing her little brother, Cole, dodging classmate Nathan Jones' wayward science lab frog and complaining about "braggamuffin" cheerleader Valentina Martinez, and the next, she and her family are fleeing for their lives to avoid dangerous flood waters. Finding a place to stay isn't easy during the disaster, and the Washington's get some surprise visitors when they finally do locate shelter. To add to the trouble, three members of the Washington family go missing during the storm, and new friends lose their home. In the middle of it all, Sophie learns to be grateful for what she has and that she is stronger than she ever imagined.

Sophie Washington: Mission Costa Rica

Welcome to the Jungle

Sixth grader Sophie Washington, her good friends, Chloe and Valentina, and her parents and brother, Cole, are in for a week of adventure when her father signs them up for a Spring Break mission trip to Costa Rica. Sophie has dreams of lazing on the beach under palm trees, but these are squashed quicker than an underfoot banana once they arrive in the rain forest and are put to work, hauling buckets of water, painting and cooking. Near the hut they sleep in, the girls fight off wayward iguanas and howler monkeys, and nightly visits from a surprise "guest" make it hard for them to get much rest after their work is done.

A wrong turn in the jungle, midway through the week, makes Sophie wish she could leave South America and join another classmate who is doing a Spring Break vacation in Disney World.

In between the daily chores the family has fun times zip lining through the rain forest and taking an exciting river cruise in crocodile-filled waters. Sophie meets new friends during the mission week who show her a different side of life, and by the end of the trip, she starts to see Costa Rica as a home away from home.

About the Author

Tonya Duncan Ellis is the author of the Sophie Washington book series: *Queen of the Bee, The Snitch, Things You Didn't Know About Sophie, The Gamer* and *Hurricane*. She also writes feature articles for family magazines. Growing up, her favorite video game was Ms. Pac-Man Tonya lives with her husband and three children in Houston, TX.